200PARADIDDLE
EXERCISESFORDRUMS

SERKAN**SÜER**

FUNDAMENTAL**CHANGES**

200 Paradiddle Exercises For Drums

Paradiddle Exercises, Grooves, Beats and Fills To Improve Drum Technique

By Serkan Suer

Published by **www.fundamental-changes.com**

ISBN: 978-1-78933-007-6

Fundamental Changes Ltd.

www.fundamental-changes.com

Cover Image Copyright Shutterstock: Milosz Aniol

Contents

Introduction

Paradiddles are popular rudiments that are frequently used in drum fills, beats and solo phrases. They are essential patterns for any drummer who wants to expand their vocabulary and drum technique and they form a fundamental part of any drummer's musical language.

Many drums teachers testify to the fact that while students often pick up the drum rudiments fairly quickly, most struggle with how to apply them to the whole kit in order to create effective grooves and fills.

This book contains over 200 examples that teach you the four basic paradiddles, but also their musical applications. It is designed for beginner-to-intermediate drum students with a basic knowledge of rhythmic theory and drum technique (single stroke notes, double stroke notes, basic drum beats, flams and drags).

There are various types of paradiddle and mastering each one will develop your musical and technical skills in different ways. The four basic patterns of the paradiddle rudiments family we will be studying are:

1. Single Paradiddle

2. Double Paradiddle

3. Single Paradiddle-diddle

4. Triple Paradiddle

By working through this book and incorporating these paradiddles into your playing, you will quickly gain new insights into rhythm, phrasing and musicality

How this book is organised

Each chapter has two main elements:

• Theoretical explanations and definitions

• Notated and recorded examples to help you build solid drumming technique

What you will learn

The 200+ examples in this drum method book will teach you to…

• Learn and internalise each paradiddle through musical examples

• Learn how to apply each paradiddle in drum beats and fills

• Develop your technique, coordination, fluency, creativity and endurance on drums

• Perform with other musicians confidently

• Develop the skills needed for self-study

• Read drum notation more easily

I am confident that if you read and practise this book in its entirety, you will quickly take your playing to a much higher level.

I wish you good luck in your drumming journey. Enjoy the book!

Serkan Süer

Halifax, N.S., Canada; April 2018

Important Study Suggestions

Read everything in the book! You will probably find diving into the examples more attractive than reading carefully through each chapter before you start playing. Please read the short theory sections or you may miss important information, tips and definitions. To get the most out of your practice time I strongly recommend that you read the book in its entirety.

Use a metronome. Practising with a metronome will help you develop your skills more quickly. The initial tempo for each example is 45 bpm (beats per minute). Once you are comfortable with an exercise and playing it accurately, then increase your speed, but gradually and incrementally. In 4/4, each click should be a 1/4th note. In 6/8, each click should be a 1/8 note.

Practise regularly. Practising exercises everyday (for at least 45 minutes) will quickly increase your overall development. If you can't create time every day, try to practise at least twice a week.

Repeat the examples again and again. While training, repetition is important. Play each exercise at different tempos to improve your skills and establish *muscle memory*. Practise each groove example repeatedly while using different ride pattern surfaces (closed hi-hats, open hi-hats, ride cymbal, floor tom, cowbell, etc.) and different snare drum options (cross-stick or rim-shot beats).

Listen to the audio while practising. Hearing the audio will help you learn the examples more easily.

Create your own exercises. After finishing each section, get creative and write your own variations. This will help you "get inside" drumming, and develop a much deeper understanding of the music. Drum beat examples in this book are written with closed hi-hats. You can also play each beat pattern on other surfaces such as the ride cymbal, crash cymbal, cowbell, floor tom etc.

Play the opposite hand combinations: start each example with your weaker hand. Hand combinations are given for some examples in the book. If you are a left-handed drummer, or you are a right-handed drummer and you want to develop your technique, then practise the examples with the opposite leading hand combinations.

Practise the "push-pull" technique. Learning the *push-pull technique* will help you play consistent double strokes which is an indispensable part of paradiddle technique, especially at faster tempos. This technique is also useful for playing double strokes evenly on different surfaces (especially on toms).

Each hand makes one downward stroke motion. Push/drop the stick to produce a bounce on the surface. Your fingers control the number of bounces. After the first bounce, pull the stick back with your fingers and wrists. Hit the second note during this upward motion.

This technique is also useful for performing paradiddles with flams at faster tempos. Again, each hand makes one downward stroke motion. You push/drop the stick to produce two bounces (a double stroke) on the surface.

After the second bounce, pull the stick back with your fingers and wrists. Hit the third note (the grace note of a flam) during this upward motion. You can build this technique by practising regularly with a metronome.

Notation key: The notation used in this book is as follows:

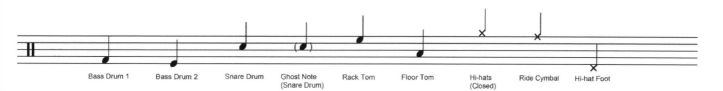

Bass Drum 1   Bass Drum 2   Snare Drum   Ghost Note (Snare Drum)   Rack Tom   Floor Tom   Hi-hats (Closed)   Ride Cymbal   Hi-hat Foot

Get the Audio

The audio files for this book are available to download for free from **www.fundamental-changes.com** and the link is in the top right corner. Simply select this book title from the drop-down menu and follow the instructions to get the audio.

We recommend that you download the files directly to your computer, not to your tablet, and extract them there before adding them to your media library. You can then put them on your tablet, iPod or burn them to CD. On the download page there is a help PDF and we also provide technical support via the contact form.

Kindle / eReaders

To get the most out of this book, remember that you can double tap any image to enlarge it. Turn off "column viewing" and hold your kindle in landscape mode.

Twitter: **@guitar_joseph**

FB: **FundamentalChangesInGuitar**

Instagram: **FundamentalChanges**

1. Single Paradiddle

The single paradiddle is one of the most common and important drum rudiments and is often played in drum beats, fills and solo phrases. Mastering this rudiment will help you develop your drumming technique, creativity, fluency and endurance on the entire drum kit.

Paradiddle refers to two alternated single strokes (R L or L R) and one double stroke (R R or L L) played respectively. Each alternating single stroke part is called a "para" and each double stroke part is called a "diddle". A single paradiddle consists of two single strokes and one double stroke. The sticking pattern of a single paradiddle roll is R L R R – L R L L and the first single stroke notes are accented.

The first example shows the 1/16th note single paradiddle. First, practise on your snare drum at slower tempos (50-60 bpm). Then, speed up gradually.

Example 1:

Moving the accented notes is a common way to create variations of the single paradiddle. Here are some examples.

Example 2:

Example 3:

Example 4:

Example 5:

Example 6:

Example 7:

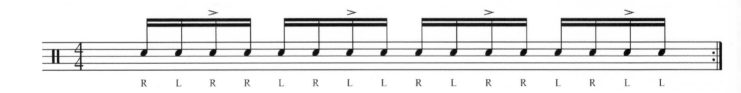

Example 8:

Single Paradiddle Drum Fills

Next, you will learn how to use the single paradiddle in great sounding *drum fills* on the entire kit. Practising the creative ideas below will improve your coordination, fluency and creativity on the whole drum kit.

• The accented notes are hit on the cymbals (w/bass drum). The remaining notes are played on the snare drum:

Example 9: The single paradiddle.

Example 10: The single paradiddle variation.

Example 11: The single paradiddle variation.

• The accented notes are hit on the floor tom or the rack tom. The remaining notes are played on snare drum:

Example 12: The single paradiddle.

Example 13: The single paradiddle variation.

R L R R L R L L R L R R L R L L

Example 14: The single paradiddle variation.

R L R R L R L L R L R R L R L L

• The single paradiddle is played between the floor tom and the rack tom:

Example 15: The single paradiddle.

R L R R L R L L R L R R L R L L

Example 16: The single paradiddle variation.

R L R R L R L L R L R R L R L L

Example 17: The single paradiddle variation.

R L R R L R L L R L R R L R L L

• The accented notes are hit on the snare drum. The remaining notes are played between the floor tom and rack tom:

Example 18: The single paradiddle.

Example 19: The single paradiddle variation.

Example 20: The single paradiddle variation.

Single Paradiddle Drum Beats

It's great to use single paradiddle ideas as *drum beats*. These beats can be used in rock, funk, pop, rap, jazz-fusion and many more styles.

Here are some single paradiddle beat examples. In each example, the ride pattern is played on the closed hi-hats and the backbeat is hit on beats 2 and 4.

Example 21:

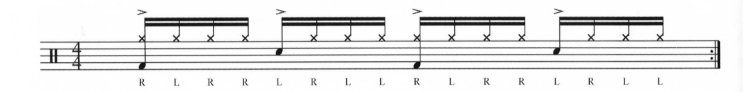

Example 22:

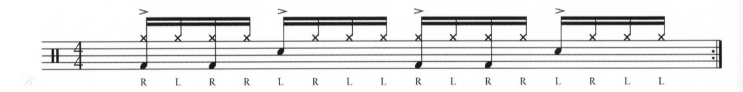

Example 23:

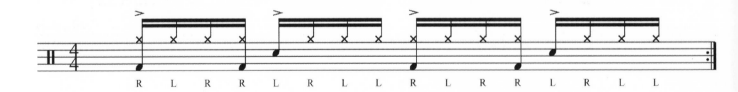

The next example demonstrates a half-time single paradiddle drum beat. The ride pattern is played on the closed hi-hats and the single backbeat is struck on beat 3.

Example 24:

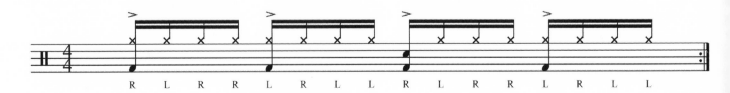

Ghost notes usually add a cool, funky feel to the single paradiddle drum beats. These sound better if the ghost notes are played softer.

In each of the following examples, the single paradiddle is played between the closed hi-hats and the snare drum with the backbeats hit on beats 2 and 4. The remaining snare drum notes are played as ghost notes. Before playing these examples, listen to the audio tracks and hear how they sound in action.

Example 25:

Example 26:

Example 27:

Inverted Paradiddle

The *inverted paradiddle* is an inversion of the single paradiddle rudiment. The double stroke (diddle) beats are moved to the middle of each paradiddle to create the inverted paradiddle. The sticking pattern is R L L R – L R R L.

Here are two different variations of the inverted paradiddle. In each variation, the accents are on different beats. Take your time while practising these on the snare drum.

Example 28: Variation 1.

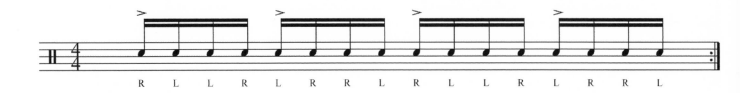

Example 29: Variation 2.

It's a good idea to practise the single paradiddle and inverted paradiddle together in the same bar.

Example 30:

Learning the inverted paradiddle will help you to improve your coordination and access interesting ideas for drum fill and groove construction.

Check out the following inverted paradiddle fills.

Example 31:

R L L R L R R L R L L R L R R L

Example 32:

R L L R L R R L R L L R L R R L

Example 33:

R L L R L R R L R L L R L R R L

Example 34:

R L L R L R R L R L L R L R R L

The next example shows a basic drum beat created from the inverted paradiddle. The ride pattern is played on the closed hi-hats and the backbeats are on 2 and 4.

Pay attention to the sticking pattern.

Example 35:

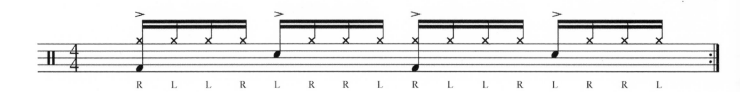

The next inverted paradiddle beat is played between the closed hi-hats and the snare drum with the backbeats on 2 and 4.

The remaining snare drum notes are played as ghost notes.

Example 36:

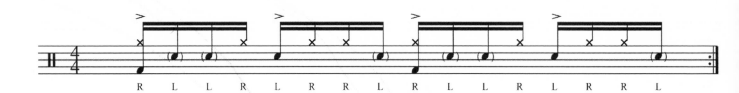

Reversed Single Paradiddle

When you move the double stroke (diddle) beats to the beginning of each paradiddle, you create a *reversed single paradiddle* sticking pattern: R R L R – L L R L.

Example 37:

As you can see in the examples below, it is possible to create cool drum fills from the reversed single paradiddle.

Example 38:

Example 39:

Flam Paradiddle

The *flam paradiddle* is a combination of two drum rudiments: the single paradiddle and the flam. It is a spiced-up version of the 1/16th note single paradiddle with grace notes. The first stroke of each paradiddle is played as a flam.

Example 40:

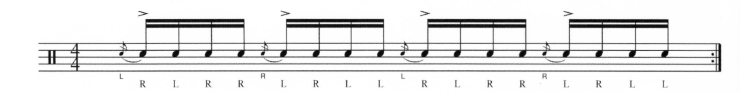

The next example will help develop your fluency and endurance on the kit. It is a flam paradiddle fill that you can use in grooves.

The primary notes are struck on the floor tom and small tom respectively on each count. The remaining notes are played on the snare drum.

Example 41:

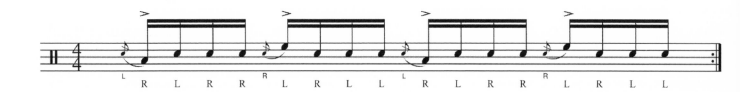

The final flam paradiddle example is a basic half-time drum beat. The primary note is hit on the snare drum as a single backbeat on count 3. The remaining notes are played on the closed hi-hats as a ride pattern.

After practising this example, try to create your own flam paradiddle beats with different snare and bass drum variations.

Example 42:

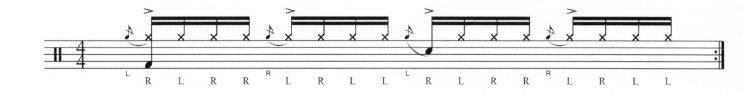

Single Flammed Mill

The next flam rudiment we will study is the *single flammed mill*. This rudiment is based on an inversion of the single paradiddle, also known as a "single mill".

A single mill consists of a double stroke and two alternating single strokes, which is played as R R L R or L L R L. Contrary to the reversed single paradiddle, the accents are on the first beat of each double stroke (diddle).

This is how the single mill is notated.

Example 43:

When you're confident with the 1/16th note single mill pattern, it's time to learn the single flammed mill. Grace notes are added to the pattern and the first note of each single mill is played as a flam.

Example 44:

Now, let's learn a drum fill constructed from the single flammed fill. Play the whole rudiment between the floor tom and the rack tom without changing your hand position.

Example 45:

The next drum beat is based on a simple idea: the single flammed mill is played between the closed hi-hats and the snare drum with the backbeats hit on beats 2 and 4. The remaining snare drum notes are played as ghost notes.

Listening to the audio track will help you understand the groove more easily.

Example 46:

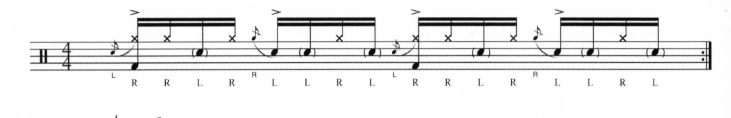

Single Dragadiddle

The *single dragadiddle* is the final rudiment based on the single paradiddle. This rudiment is a 1/16th note single paradiddle starting with a drag (1/32nd note double stroke). The drag is indicated with a short line on the stem of each accented note.

Learn how to play the single dragadiddle.

Example 47:

Now, check out this cool single dragadiddle fill. The drags are hit on the floor tom and the small tom respectively on each count. The remaining notes of the rudiment are played on the snare drum.

Example 48:

The following example demonstrates a half-time drum beat created with the single dragadiddle. The ride pattern is played on the closed hi-hats and the single backbeat (a drag) is struck on beat 3.

Example 49:

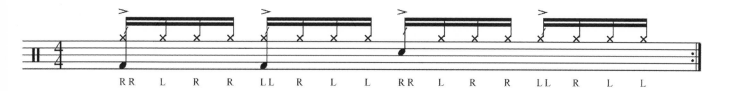

As well as the single dragadiddle rudiment, you can also play drags with the single paradiddle in various combinations.

Here is a creative example.

Example 50:

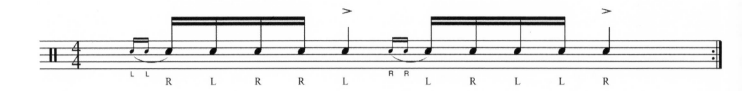

Single Paradiddle Feet Patterns

You can create and play interesting *single paradiddle feet patterns* to build up your foot technique, pace and balance on the drum kit.

There are four basic ideas and examples shown here. Examine each idea and groove carefully.

• The single paradiddle roll is played between the bass drum and the hi-hat foot pedal. The backbeats are hit on beat 2 and beat 4.

Example 51:

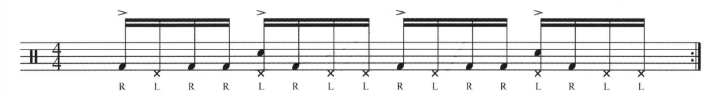

• The single paradiddle roll is played between the bass drum 1 and bass drum 2. The backbeats are hit on beat 2 and beat 4.

Example 52:

• The single paradiddle roll is played between the bass drum 1 and bass drum 2. The backbeats are hit on beat 2 and beat 4. The 1/4 note ride cymbal beats are added to the groove.

Example 53:

• The single paradiddle roll is played between the bass drum 1 and bass drum 2. The backbeats are hit on beat 2 and beat 4. The 1/8th note ride cymbal beats are added to the groove.

Example 54:

2. Double Paradiddle

The double paradiddle is the second main paradiddle rudiment. It has a 1/16th note sextuplet structure and comprises of four alternating single strokes and one double stroke.

The sticking pattern of a double paradiddle roll is R L R L R R – L R L R L L and the first single stroke note is accented.

The notation of the double paradiddle rudiment is shown below.

Example 55:

Now let's examine some variations of the double paradiddle. When you take a closer look at these variations, you will notice that the accented notes are moved each time.

Take your time and perform these snare drum exercises accurately.

Example 56:

Example 57:

Example 58:

R L R L R R L R L R L L L R L R L R R L R L R L L L

Example 59:

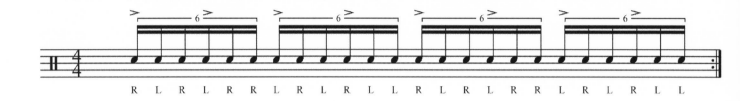

R L R L R R L R L R L L L R L R L R R L R L R L L L

Example 60:

R L R L R R L R L R L L L R L R L R R L R L R L L L

Example 61:

R L R L R R L R L R L L L R L R L R R L R L R L L L

Double Paradiddle Drum Fills

The double paradiddle rudiment can be used to construct many colourful drum fills. Here are some creative ideas and fill examples. Practise these examples to develop endurance and pace in your drumming.

• The accented notes are hit on the cymbals (w/bass drum). The remaining notes are played on the snare drum:

Example 62: The double paradiddle.

Example 63: The double paradiddle variation.

Example 64: The double paradiddle variation.

• The accented notes are hit on the floor tom or rack tom. The remaining notes are played on snare drum:

Example 65: The double paradiddle.

Example 66: The double paradiddle variation.

R L R L R R L R L R L L R L R L R R L R L R L L

Example 67: The double paradiddle variation.

R L R L R R L R L R L L R L R L R R L R L R L L

• The single paradiddle is played fully between the floor tom and the rack tom:

Example 68: The double paradiddle.

R L R L R R L R L R L L R L R L R R L R L R L L

Example 69: The double paradiddle variation.

R L R L R R L R L R L L R L R L R R L R L R L L

Example 70: The double paradiddle variation.

• The accented notes are hit on the snare drum. The remaining notes are played between the floor tom and rack tom:

Example 71: The double paradiddle.

Example 72: The double paradiddle variation.

Example 73: The double paradiddle variation.

Double Paradiddle Drum Beats

Applying the double paradiddle sticking pattern to drum beats is a fun way of building your technique. In each drum beat below, the ride pattern is played on the closed hi-hats and the backbeats are hit on beats 2 and 4.

Example 74:

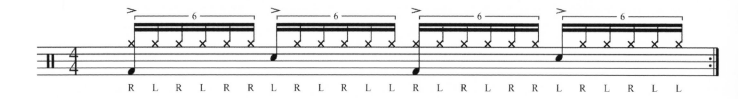

Example 75:

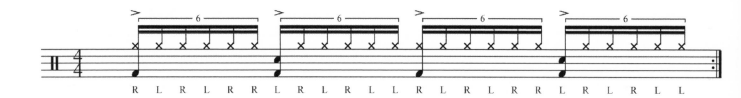

Example 76:

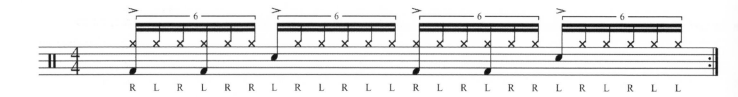

The next example is played in half time The 1/16th note sextuplet ride pattern is played on the closed hi-hats and the single backbeat is struck on beat 3.

Example 77:

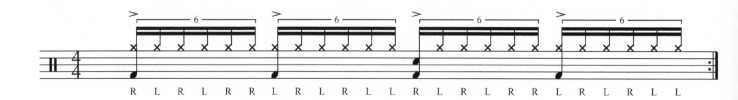

Now, check out this interesting double paradiddle beat with a double-time feel.

Example 78:

The following examples will help you to develop your technical command over double paradiddles, accented notes and ghost notes at the same time.

Example 79:

Example 80:

Example 81:

Double Paradiddle with Flams and Drags

Although there are no specific sticking patterns identified in the 40 main drum rudiments, you should still gain the technical ability of adding *flams* and *drags* to the double paradiddle. Let's have a look at these first examples.

Example 82: The double paradiddle is played with flams.

Example 83: The double paradiddle is played with drags.

Reversed Double Paradiddle

When you move the double stroke (diddle) notes to the beginning of each double paradiddle, this re-arranged sticking pattern is called a *reversed single paradiddle*: R R L R L R – L L R L R L. Here's how it looks on paper:

Example 84:

As shown in the next two examples, you can use the reversed double paradiddle pattern as drum fills.

Example 85:

Example 86:

If the accents of a reversed double paradiddle are played on the first note of each double stroke (diddle), this new transition is called a *double mill*.

Example 87:

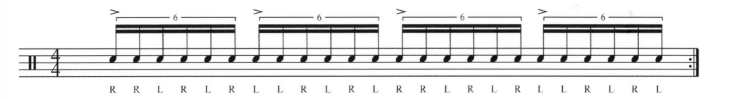

Drag Paradiddle #1

The *drag paradiddle #1* is an interesting rudiment based on the double paradiddle. This rudiment is written in 6/8-time signature and consists of an accented 1/8th note single stroke and a 1/16th note paradiddle. The drag is played just before the paradiddle.

There is an easy way to play the drag paradiddle #1: first, play a double paradiddle (R L R L R R / L R L R L L). Then, play a drag instead of each second 1/16th note (R LL R L R R / L RR L R L L).

Concentrate on the notation and listen to the audio track to execute this rudiment correctly.

Example 88:

The next example shows a melodic drag paradiddle #1 fill. The accented notes are hit on the floor tom and the rack tom respectively. The remaining notes are played on the snare drum.

Example 89:

Here is a bluesy 6/8-drum beat created with the drag paradiddle #1. The ride pattern is played on the closed hi-hats. On count 4, the accented note is struck on the snare drum.

Example 90:

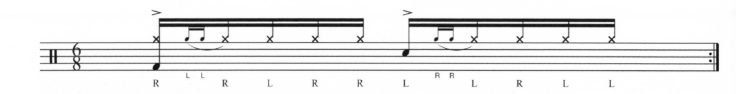

Double Paradiddle Feet Patterns

We will complete this chapter by practising *double paradiddle feet patterns*.

Here are four challenging ideas. Practise them slowly with a metronome and don't speed up until you can play them smoothly.

• The double paradiddle roll is played between the bass drum and the hi-hat foot pedal. The backbeats are hit on beat 2 and beat 4.

Example 91:

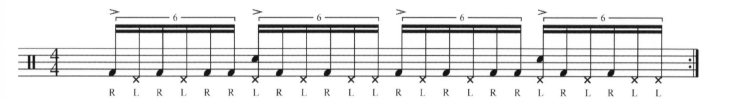

• The double paradiddle roll is played between the bass drum 1 and bass drum 2. The backbeats are hit on beat 2 and beat 4.

Example 92:

• The double paradiddle roll is played between the bass drum 1 and bass drum 2. The backbeats are hit on beat 2 and beat 4. The 1/4 note ride cymbal beats are added to the groove.

Example 93:

• The double paradiddle roll is played between the bass drum 1 and bass drum 2. The backbeats are hit on beat 2 and beat 4. The 1/8th note ride cymbal beats are added to the groove.

Example 94:

R L R L R R L R L R L L R L R L R R L R L R L L

3. Single Paradiddle-diddle

After mastering the single and double paradiddle rudiments in the previous chapters, it's time to study the *single paradiddle-diddle*. It has a 1/16th note sextuplet structure and consists of two alternating single strokes and two alternating double strokes. The first single strokes are accented.

The hand combination of the single paradiddle-diddle doesn't naturally alternate within itself. To develop your technique, you should practise these examples leading with each hand. If you naturally lead with your right, make sure to practise leading with your left too.

The sticking pattern of the single paradiddle-diddle is shown in the following example. Practise it at slower tempos (50–60 bpm) until you can play it fluently. Then speed up gradually and build to faster tempos.

Example 95:

Next, the accented notes of the single paradiddle-diddle are shifted to enhance the rudiment and create the following variations.

Example 96:

Example 97:

Example 98:

R L R R L L R L R R L L R L R R L L R L R R L L

Example 99:

R L R R L L R L R R L L R L R R L L R L R R L L

Single Paradiddle-diddle Drum Fills

Now you will learn how to apply the single paradiddle-diddle to drum fills. The following creative ideas and drum fills are important additions to your drumming repertoire.

• The accented notes are hit on the cymbals (w/bass drum). The remaining notes are played on the snare drum:

Example 100: The single paradiddle-diddle.

Example 101: The single paradiddle-diddle variation.

Example 102: The single paradiddle-diddle variation.

• The accented notes are hit on the floor tom or rack tom. The remaining notes are played on snare drum:

Example 103: The single paradiddle-diddle.

Example 104: The single paradiddle-diddle variation.

Example 105: The single paradiddle-diddle variation.

• The single paradiddle is fully played between the floor tom and the rack tom:

Example 106: The single paradiddle-diddle.

Example 107: The single paradiddle-diddle variation.

R L R R L L R L R R L L R L R R L L R L R R L L

Example 108: The single paradiddle-diddle variation.

R L R R L L R L R R L L R L R R L L R L R R L L

• The accented notes are hit on the snare drum. The remaining notes are played between the floor tom and rack tom:

Example 109: The single paradiddle-diddle.

R L R R L L R L R R L L R L R R L L R L R R L L

Example 110: The single paradiddle-diddle variation.

R L R R L L R L R R L L R L R R L L R L R R L L

Example 111: The single paradiddle-diddle variation.

R L R R L L R L R R L L R L R R L L R L R R L L

Single Paradiddle-diddle Drum Beats

The next three single paradiddle-diddle patterns are fairly straightforward drum beats. In each example the ride pattern is played on the closed hi-hats. Pay attention to the bass drum and snare drum variations.

Example 112:

Example 113:

Example 114:

The example below is a cool half-time drum beat. Once again, the ride pattern is played on the closed hi-hats and the single backbeat is hit on beat 3.

Example 115:

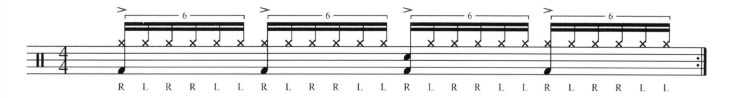

The following patterns are funky drum beats that are enhanced with ghost notes. Technically, these examples are more complicated than the previous examples, so you may need to spend more time practising them.

In each example, the single paradiddle-diddle is played between the closed hi-hats and the snare drum.

Example 116:

Example 117:

Reversed Single Paradiddle-diddle

Next, we will check out an inversion called *the reversed single paradiddle-diddle.* This sticking pattern is created by beginning with the two double strokes and ending with the single strokes: R R L L R L.

Example 118:

You can continue building up your technical skills by using the reversed single paradiddle-diddle in drum fills.

Here are two basic variations.

Example 119:

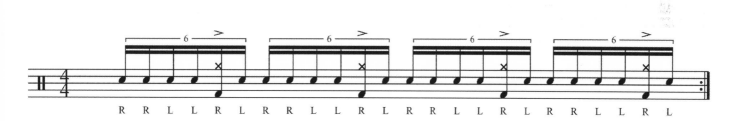

Example 120:

Flam Paradiddle-diddle

The *flam paradiddle-diddle* is a mixture of a flam and a single paradiddle-diddle rudiment. It has a 1/16th note sextuplet structure and consists of two alternating single strokes and two alternating double strokes with the first single stroke played as a flam.

You can see the notation of the flam paradiddle-diddle in the example below. Learn this rudiment leading with each hand:

Example 121:

The next example demonstrates a single flam paradiddle-diddle fill. In this fill, the primary notes on beats 1 and 2 are hit on the rack tom and the primary notes on beats 3 and 4 are struck on the floor tom. The remaining notes of the rudiment are played on the snare drum:

Example 122:

By practising the next example, you will learn how to use the flam paradiddle-diddle as a fantastic drum beat. The ride pattern (including the grace notes) is played on the closed hi-hats with two backbeats struck on counts 2 and 4:

Example 123:

Single Paradiddle-diddle Feet Patterns

Finally, let's practise the following feet patterns. Applying the single paradiddle-diddle to feet patterns can be tricky. Be patient and use a metronome to speed up accurately

• The single paradiddle-diddle roll is played between the bass drum and the hi-hat foot pedal. The backbeats are hit on beat 2 and beat 4.

Example 124:

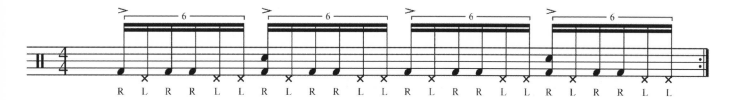

• The single paradiddle-diddle roll is played between the bass drum 1 and bass drum 2. The backbeats are hit on beat 2 and beat 4.

Example 125:

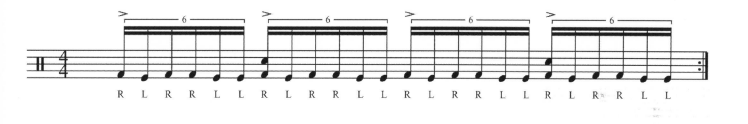

• The single paradiddle-diddle roll is played between the bass drum 1 and bass drum 2. The backbeats are hit on beat 2 and beat 4. The 1/4 note ride cymbal beats are added to the groove.

Example 126:

• The single paradiddle-diddle roll is played between the bass drum 1 and bass drum 2. The backbeats are hit on beat 2 and beat 4. The 1/8th note ride cymbal beats are added to the groove.

Example 127:

4. Triple Paradiddle

In this chapter, we will study the fourth and final pattern of the paradiddle rudiments family: *the triple paradiddle*. This rudiment has a similar structure to the single paradiddle. It comprises of six alternating single strokes and one double stroke. The first single stroke is accented.

The 1/16th note triple paradiddle is notated in the following way. Focus on the hand combination of this rudiment and try to play it evenly.

Example 128:

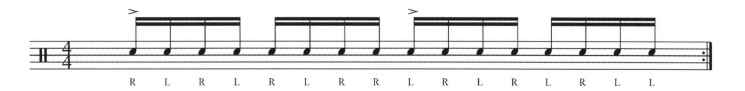

Now, check out the following triple paradiddle variations on the snare drum. As you will notice, the accents are played on different beats.

Example 129:

Example 130:

Example 131:

R L R L R L R L R R L R L R L R L L

Example 132:

R L R L R L R L R R L R L R L R L L

Example 133:

R L R L R L R L R R L R L R L R L L

Triple Paradiddle Drum Fills

It is important for your technical progress to create and play triple paradiddle drum fills. You should already be familiar with the creative ideas below from previous chapters. Now, you will develop them as triple paradiddle fills. As always, read the explanations and listen to the audio tracks before starting your practice.

• The accented notes are hit on the cymbals (w/bass drum). The remaining notes are played on the snare drum:

Example 134: The triple paradiddle.

Example 135: The triple paradiddle variation.

Example 136: The triple paradiddle variation.

• The accented notes are played on the floor tom or the rack tom. The remaining notes are played on snare drum:

Example 137: The triple paradiddle.

Example 138: The triple paradiddle variation.

R L R L R L R R L R L R L R L L

Example 139: The triple paradiddle variation.

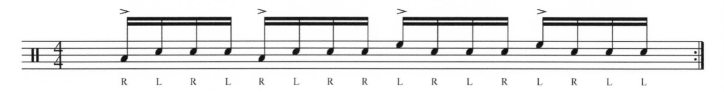

R L R L R L R R L R L R L R L L

• The single paradiddle is played entirely between the floor tom and rack tom:

Example 140: The triple paradiddle.

R L R L R L R R L R L R L R L L

Example 141: The triple paradiddle variation.

R L R L R L R R L R L R L R L L

Example 142: The triple paradiddle variation.

R L R L R L R R L R L R L R L L

• The accented notes are hit on the snare drum. The remaining notes are played between the floor tom and rack tom:

Example 143: The triple paradiddle.

R L R L R L R R L R L R L R L L

Example 144: The triple paradiddle variation.

R L R L R L R R L R L R L R L L

Example 145: The triple paradiddle variation.

R L R L R L R R L R L R L R L L

Triple Paradiddle Drum Beats

After mastering the triple paradiddle fills, the next step is to practise it in drum beats. The following three examples demonstrate half-time drum beats with different bass drum patterns.

In each example, the ride pattern is played on the closed hi-hats and the single backbeat is struck on beat 3.

Example 146:

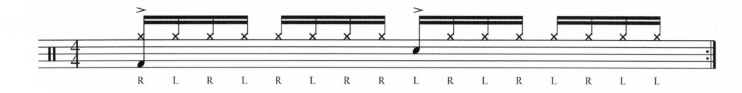

Example 147:

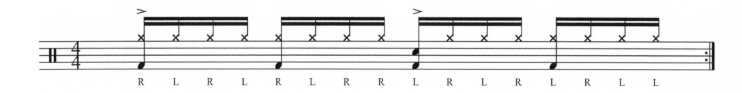

Example 148:

You can continue to improve your coordination and fluency with the triple paradiddle pattern by practising the following groove variations. This time the backbeats are hit on beats 2 and 4.

Example 149:

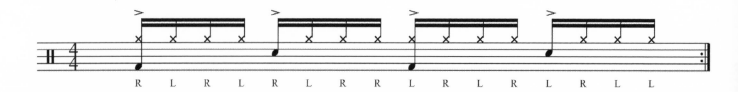

Example 150:

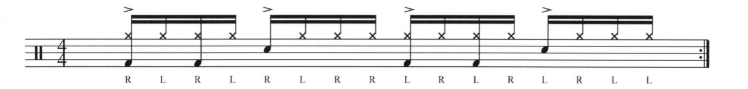

Example 151:

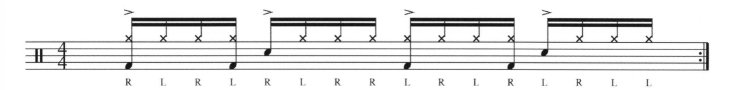

Adding ghost notes into grooves is an important technique for creating colourful sounding drum beats.

In the following half-time drum beat, the triple paradiddle is played between the closed hi-hats and the snare drum. The accented backbeats are struck on counts 2 and 4. The remaining snare drum notes are played as ghost notes.

Example 152:

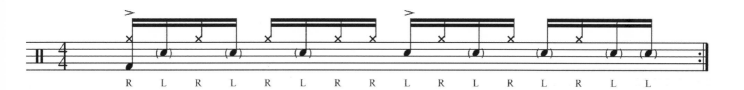

Reversed Triple Paradiddle

Now let's study the *reversed triple paradiddle.* The sticking pattern of this inversion begins with the double stroke notes: R R L R L R L R – L L R L R L R L.

Example 153:

Once you can perform the reversed triple paradiddle fluently on the snare drum, you can try the following drum fills.

Example 154:

Example 155:

Triple Paradiddle with 'Flams' and 'Drags'

There are two different examples for you in this section. The first shows a combination of the triple paradiddle and flams. The second demonstrates a two-bar phrase combination of the triple paradiddle and drags.

Paying attention to the audio tracks and practising regularly will help you learn these patterns quickly.

Example 156: The triple paradiddle is played with flams.

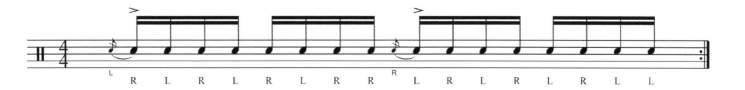

Example 157: The triple paradiddle is played with drags in a two-bar phrase.

Drag Paradiddle #2

Another drag rudiment based on the paradiddle is the *drag paradiddle #2*. Technically, it comprises an 1/8th note double stroke and a 1/16th note paradiddle. The first drag is played before the second 1/8th note stroke and the second drag is played just before the paradiddle. The first note is accented.

You can follow these steps to learn this rudiment quickly: first, play a triple paradiddle (R L R L R L R R / L R L R L R L L). Then, play drags instead of each second and fourth 1/16 note (R LL R LL R L R R / L RR L RR L R L L). Examine the hand combination and practise it with a metronome.

Example 158:

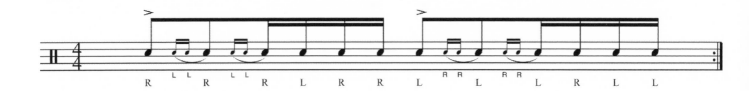

The following fill is created with a simple idea based around the drag paradiddle #2. The accented notes are struck on the floor tom and the rack tom respectively. The remaining notes (including the drags) of the rudiment are played on the snare drum.

Example 159:

Finally, let's try this funky beat created with drag paradiddle #2. Once more, the ride pattern is played on the closed hi-hats with a backbeat struck on count 3.

Example 160:

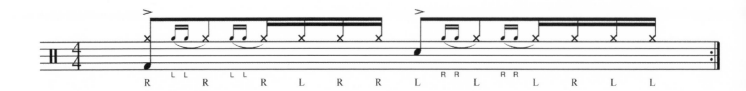

Triple Paradiddle Feet Patterns

We will finish this chapter by learning four triple paradiddle feet patterns.

• The triple paradiddle roll is played between the bass drum and the hi-hat foot pedal. The single backbeat is hit on beat 3.

Example 161:

• The triple paradiddle roll is played between the bass drum 1 and bass drum 2. The single backbeat is hit on beat 3.

Example 162:

• The triple paradiddle roll is played between the bass drum 1 and bass drum 2. The single backbeat is hit on beat 3. The 1/4 note ride cymbal beats are added to the groove.

Example 163:

• The triple paradiddle roll is played between the bass drum 1 and bass drum 2. The single backbeat is hit on beat 3. The 1/8th note ride cymbal beats are added to the groove.

Example 164:

5. Mixed Paradiddle Exercises

When you have mastered all four fundamental paradiddle rudiments, you are ready to combine them into two-bar and four-bar phrases. Practising *mixed paradiddle exercises* will not only elevate your technical skill, it will also add musicality and creativity to your drumming. You can play each example in grooves or drum solos.

Playing two-bar and four-bar paradiddle phrases is quite challenging, so read the explanations, listen to the audio tracks and practise each example carefully with a metronome.

Two-Bar Mixed Paradiddle Exercises

In this section, you will discover creative ideas that combine different paradiddles in two-bar phrases.

• The following two-bar phrase combinations are created with the single paradiddle and double paradiddle:

Example 165: The single paradiddle is in bar one. The double paradiddle is in bar two.

Example 166: The single paradiddle fill is in bar one. The double paradiddle fill is in bar two.

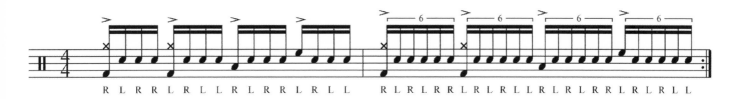

Example 167: The single paradiddle variation is in bar one. The double paradiddle variation is in bar two.

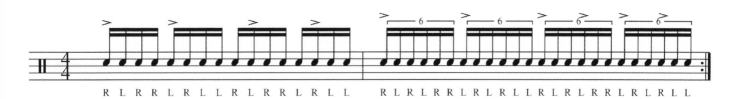

Example 168: The single paradiddle fill variation is in bar one. The double paradiddle fill variation is in bar two.

Example 169: The flam paradiddle is in bar one. The double paradiddle with flams is in bar two.

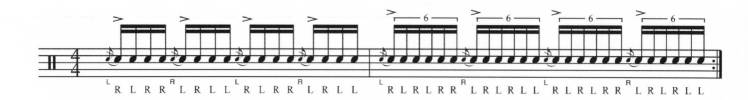

Example 170: The flam paradiddle fill is in bar one. The double paradiddle fill with flams is in bar two.

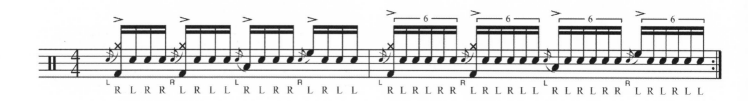

Example 171: The single paradiddle drum beat is in bar one. The double paradiddle drum beat is in bar two.

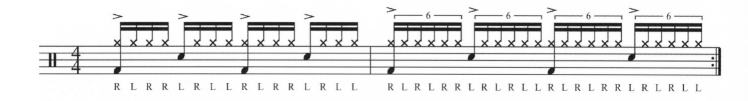

• The following two-bar phrase combinations are created with the single paradiddle and single paradiddle-diddle:

Example 172: The single paradiddle is in bar one. The single paradiddle-diddle is in bar two.

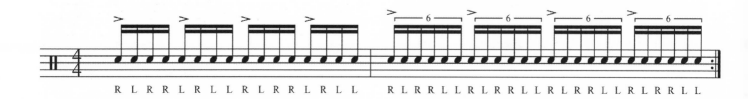

Example 173: The single paradiddle fill is in bar one. The single paradiddle-diddle fill is in bar two.

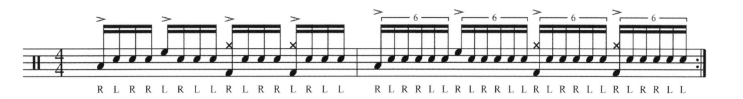

Example 174: The single paradiddle variation is in bar one. The single paradiddle-diddle variation is in bar two.

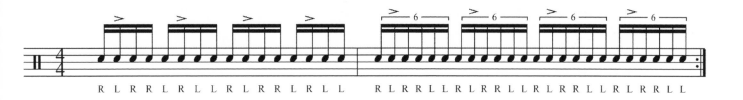

Example 175: The single paradiddle fill variation is in bar one. The single paradiddle-diddle fill variation is in bar two.

Example 176: The flam paradiddle is in bar one. The flam paradiddle-diddle is in bar two.

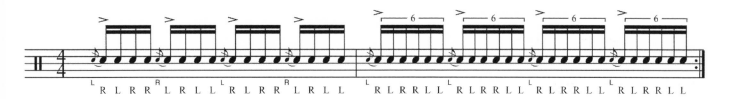

Example 177: The flam paradiddle fill is in bar one. The flam paradiddle-diddle fill is in bar two.

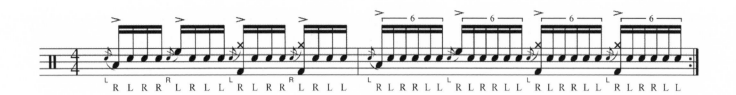

Example 178: The single paradiddle drum beat is in bar one. The single paradiddle-diddle drum beat is in bar two.

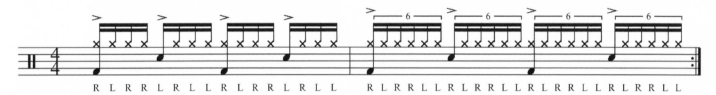

• The following two-bar phrase combinations are created with the single paradiddle and the triple paradiddle:

Example 179: The single paradiddle is in bar one; the triple paradiddle is in bar two.

Example 180: The single paradiddle fill is in bar one. The triple paradiddle fill is in bar two.

Example 181: The single paradiddle variation is in bar one. The triple paradiddle variation is in bar two.

R L R R L R L L L R L R R L R L L
R L R L R L R R L R L R L R L L

Example 182: The single paradiddle fill variation is in bar one. The triple paradiddle fill variation is in bar two.

R L R R L R L L L R L R R L R L L
R L R L R L R R L R L R L R L L

Example 183: The flam paradiddle is in bar one. The triple paradiddle with flams is in bar two.

R L R R L R L L L R L R R L R L L
R L R L R L R R L R L R L R L L

Example 184: The flam paradiddle fill is in bar one. The triple paradiddle fill with flams is in bar two.

R L R R L R L L L R L R R L R L L
R L R L R L R R L R L R L R L L

Example 185: The single paradiddle drum beat is in bar one. The triple paradiddle drum beat is in bar two.

• The following two-bar phrase combinations are created with the double paradiddle and the single paradiddle-diddle:

Example 186: The double paradiddle is in bar one. The single paradiddle-diddle is in bar two.

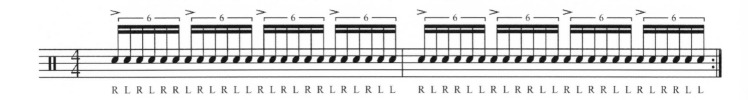

Example 187: The double paradiddle fill is in bar one. The single paradiddle-diddle fill is in bar two.

Example 188: The double paradiddle variation is in bar one. The single paradiddle-diddle variation is in bar two.

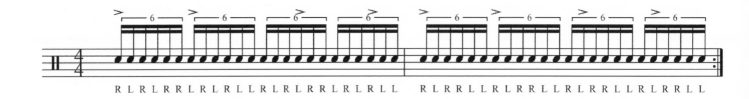

Example 189: The double paradiddle fill variation is in bar one. The single paradiddle-diddle fill variation is in bar two.

Example 190: The double paradiddle with flams is in bar one. The flam paradiddle-diddle is in bar two.

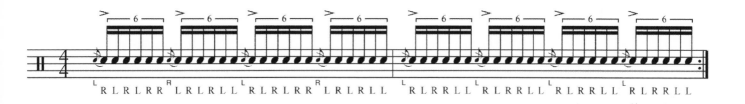

Example 191: The double paradiddle fill with flams is in bar one. The flam paradiddle-diddle fill with flams is in bar two.

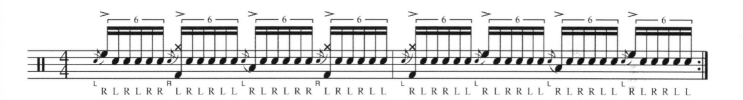

Example 192: The double paradiddle drum beat is in bar one. The single paradiddle-diddle drum beat is in bar two.

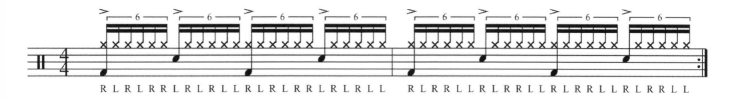

• The following two-bar phrase combinations are created with the double paradiddle and the triple paradiddle:

Example 193: The double paradiddle is in bar one. The triple paradiddle is in bar two.

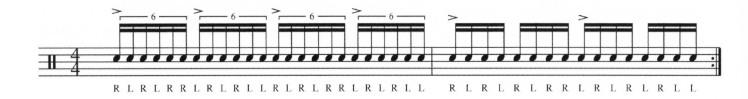

Example 194: The double paradiddle fill is in bar one. The triple paradiddle fill is in bar two.

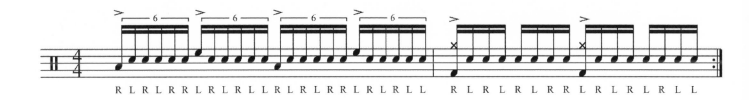

Example 195: The double paradiddle variation is in bar one. The triple paradiddle variation is in bar two.

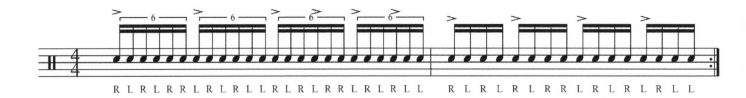

Example 196: The double paradiddle fill variation is in bar one. The triple paradiddle fill variation is in bar two.

Example 197: The double paradiddle with flams is in bar one. The triple paradiddle with flams is in bar two.

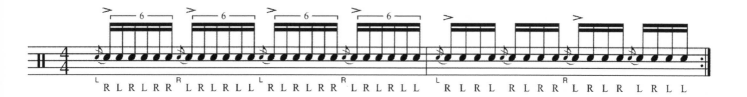

Example 198: The double paradiddle fill with flams is in bar one. The double paradiddle fill with flams is in bar two.

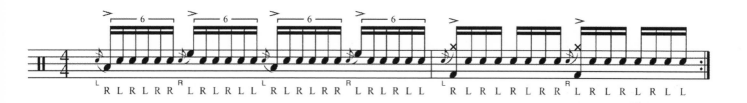

Example 199: The double paradiddle drum beat is in bar one. The triple paradiddle drum beat is in bar two.

• The following two-bar phrase combinations are created with the single paradiddle-diddle and the triple paradiddle:

Example 200: The single paradiddle-diddle is in bar one. The triple paradiddle is in bar two.

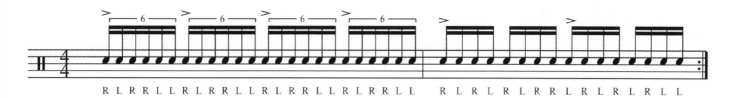

Example 201: The single paradiddle-diddle fill is in bar one. The triple paradiddle fill is in bar two.

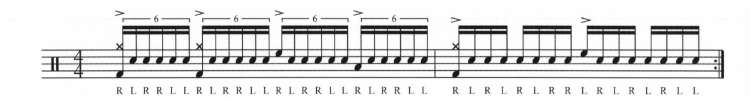

RLRRLLRLRRLLRLRRLLRLRRLL   RLRLRLRRLRLRLRLL

Example 202: The single paradiddle-diddle variation is in bar one. The triple paradiddle variation is in bar two.

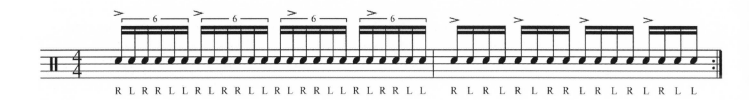

RLRRLLRLRRLLRLRRLLRLRRLL   RLRLRLRRLRLRLRLL

Example 203: The single paradiddle-diddle fill variation is in bar one. The triple paradiddle fill variation is in bar two.

RLRRLLRLRRLLRLRRLLRLRRLL   RLRLRLRRLRLRLRLL

Example 204: The flam paradiddle-diddle is in bar one. The triple paradiddle with flams is in bar two.

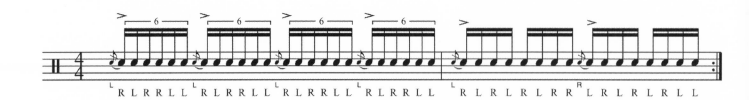

L   L   L   L   L   R
RLRRLL RLRRLL RLRRLL RLRRLL   RLRLRLRR LRLRLRLL

Example 205: The flam paradiddle-diddle fill is in bar one. The triple paradiddle fill with flams is in bar two.

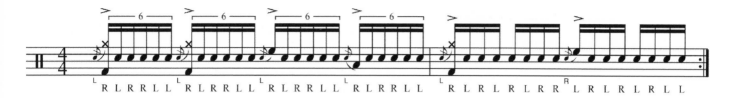

Example 206: The single paradiddle-diddle drum beat is in bar one. The triple paradiddle drum beat is in bar two.

Four-Bar Mixed Paradiddle Exercises

Now let's create four-bar phrase combinations with all four paradiddle rudiments. The following examples will help you develop your technique over paradiddles and prepare you for more complex grooves, drum fills and solos.

Example 207: The single paradiddle is in bar one. The double paradiddle is in bar two. The single paradiddle-diddle is in bar three. The triple paradiddle is in bar four.

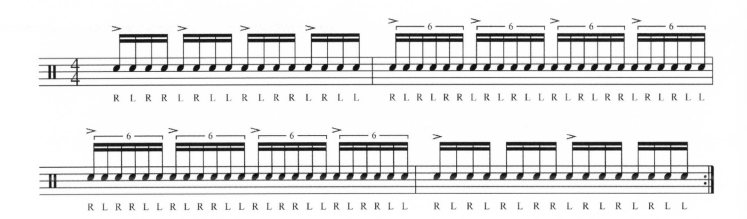

Example 208: The single paradiddle fill is in bar one. The double paradiddle fill is in bar two. The single paradiddle-diddle fill is in bar three. The triple paradiddle fill is in bar four.

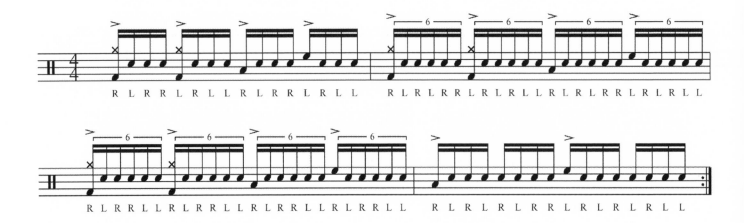

Example 209: The single paradiddle fill is in bar one. The double paradiddle fill is in bar two. The single paradiddle-diddle fill is in bar three. The triple paradiddle fill is in bar four.

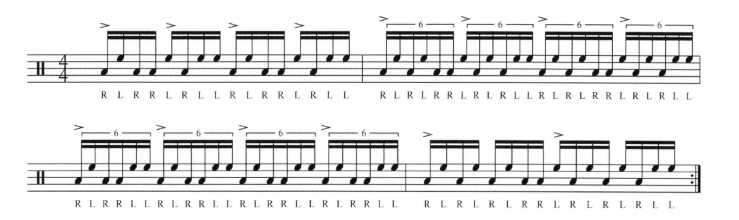

Example 210: The single paradiddle fill is in bar one. The double paradiddle fill is in bar two. The single paradiddle-diddle fill is in bar three. The triple paradiddle fill is in bar four.

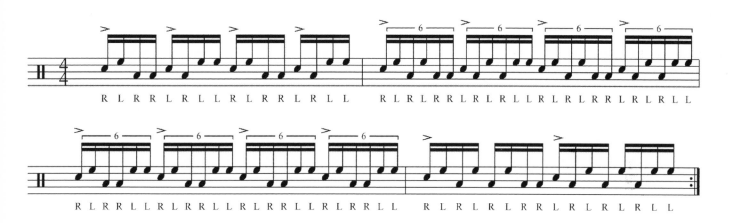

Example 211: The single paradiddle variation is in bar one. The double paradiddle variation is in bar two. The single paradiddle-diddle variation is in bar three. The triple paradiddle variation is in bar four.

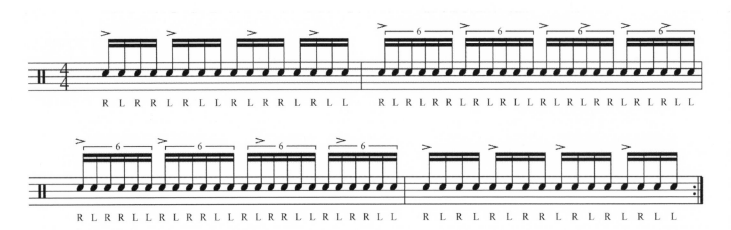

Example 212: The single paradiddle fill variation is in bar one. The double paradiddle fill variation is in bar two. The single paradiddle-diddle fill variation is in bar three. The triple paradiddle fill variation is in bar four.

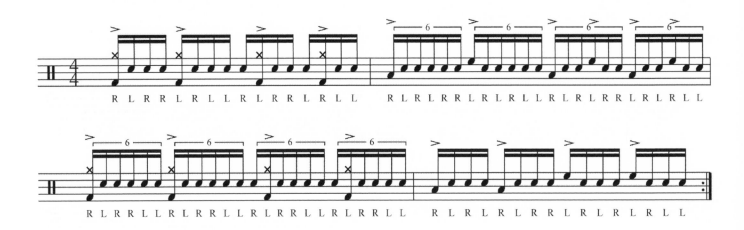

Example 213: The flam paradiddle is in bar one. The double paradiddle with flams is in bar two. The flam paradiddle-diddle is in bar three. The triple paradiddle with flams is in bar four.

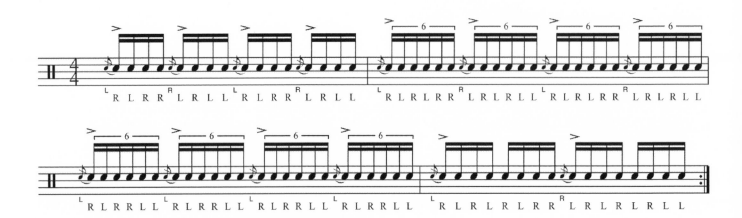

Example 214: The flam paradiddle fill is in bar one. The double paradiddle fill with flams is in bar two. The flam paradiddle-diddle fill is in bar three. The triple paradiddle fill with flams is in bar four.

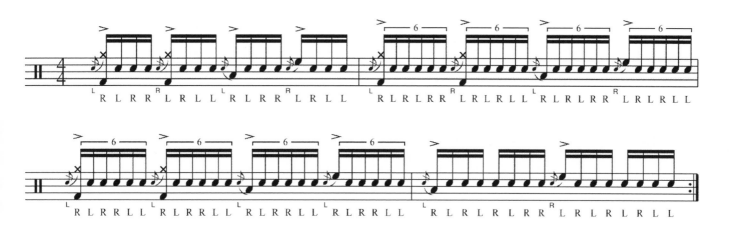

Example 215: The single paradiddle drum beat is in bar one. The double paradiddle drum beat is in bar two. The single paradiddle-diddle drum beat is in bar three. The triple paradiddle drum beat is in bar four.

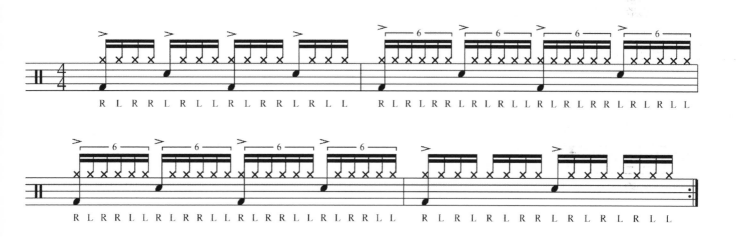

Paradiddle Cadence

The final example in this book is a specific four-bar phrase pattern called the *paradiddle cadence*. It has a 1/16th note structure and consists of four single paradiddles, four double paradiddles and three triple paradiddles.

Normally, the double paradiddle has a 1/16th note sextuplet structure. However, in the paradiddle cadence, the double paradiddles are played as 1/16th notes.

Notice that the leading hand and the sticking combinations alternate in each repeat of this four-bar phrase.

Example 216:

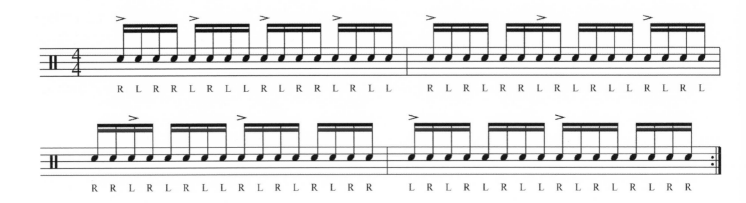

Conclusion

Congratulations on completing this book!

Now that you have mastered the theoretical knowledge, skills, musical application and techniques of paradiddle rudiments, you are ready to move on. Don't forget maintain your skills and technique by practising regularly the examples in this book.

The next step is to figure out the music that you want to play. Continue to build on the basic skills you have learnt in this book and begin to study how they can be applied to different genres such as rock, jazz, Latin, funk, blues, soul, hip-hop, etc. Exploring different types of music will influence and improve your drumming skills.

Join a band to gain experience and confidence in performing live. Being part of a band gives you the chance to hang out with other musicians, play songs you like, perform in concerts, gain musical experience and enjoy your time as a drummer.

Thank you once again for reading and working through this book. I wish you all the best in your musical journey!

I'll leave you with the following words from three great drummers:

"You can only get better by playing." – Buddy Rich.

"Playing fast around the drums is one thing. But to play music for others to listen to, that's something else. That's a whole other world." – Tony Williams.

"To me, the most important tool is not a physical or a technical one. It's more of a cerebral one. It's your brain. It's about having an interest in experimenting musically, perhaps touching on several different genres of music. No doubt, the most important tool is the mind. It's the willingness to experiment freely." – Mike Portnoy.

Have fun!

Serkan

Other Drum Books from Fundamental Changes

Drum Rudiments and Musical Application

40 essential drum rudiments have become the foundation of all modern drum technique and tuition. Every one is taught in Drum Rudiments and Musical Application.

Rhythm Reading and Notation for Drums

From basic note divisions, through to an understanding of complex time, there is an emphasis on using the correct counting, combining techniques smoothly, building great technique and developing creativity.

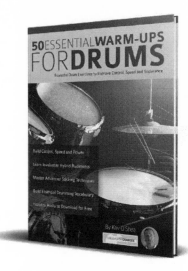

50 Essential Warm-ups for Drums

50 Essential Warm-ups for Drums teaches you the perfect method to approach every practise session, gig, or drum lesson.

Rock Drumming for Beginners

Rock Drumming for Beginners is a comprehensive course in rock drums; from basic rudiments right through to modern drum techniques.

Learn to Play Drums

Learn to Play Drums is the most in-depth guide to building modern drum technique available.